For Sue and Paul

~ A H B

For Jess

~ T W

LITTLE TIGER PRESS
An imprint of Magi Publications
1 The Coda Centre, 189 Munster Road, London SW6 6AW
www.littletigerpress.com
First published in Great Britain 1998
This edition published 2011
Text copyright © A.H. Benjamin 1998
Illustrations copyright © Tim Warnes 1998
A.H. Benjamin and Tim Warnes have asserted their rights
to be identified as the author and illustrator of this work under
the Copyright, Designs and Patents Act, 1988
A CIP catalogue record for this book is available from the British Library
All rights reserved • ISBN 978-1-84895-211-9
Printed in China • LTP/1800/0132/0211
10 9 8 7 6 5 4 3 2 1

Lucky
Little Mouse!

by A.H.Benjamin

illustrated by Tim Warnes

LITTLE TIGER PRESS
London

Mouse was on his way back home
after visiting his town cousin,
when . . .

WHOOPS!

. . .he lost his balance
and fell to the ground.

"Ouch!" said Mouse.
"This isn't my
lucky day."

But it could have
been worse!

Mouse picked himself up
and carried on his way.
He came to an open field
and was scurrying across it,
when . . .

CRASH!

. . . he fell into a hole and disappeared completely.

"Why do things *always* go wrong for me?" grumbled Mouse.

But it could have been worse!

Mouse clambered out of
the hole and was off again.

"I think I'll take a rest," he said.
Mouse had just found a nice
comfy spot, when . . .

OUCH!

. . . he sat on a thistle
and shot into the air.

"Everything happens to me!" wailed Mouse as he pulled some prickles out of his bottom.

But it could have been worse!

Mouse walked down the hill until he reached a stream. He began to cross it by stepping on the stones, when . . .

SPLASH!

...he landed
in the water.

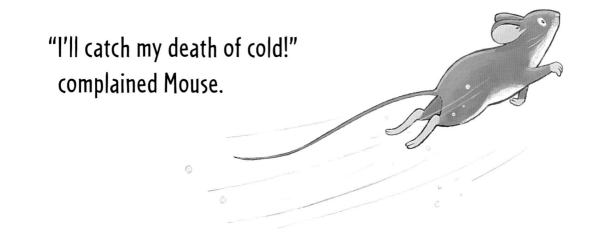

"I'll catch my death of cold!"
complained Mouse.

But it could have been worse!

Mouse paddled to the edge of the
stream and climbed out of the water.

Shaking himself dry, he was just about
to scramble down a steep bank, when . . .

WHEEE!

. . . he lost his footing and
skidded right to the bottom.

"I'll be black and blue all over," cried Mouse.

But it could have been worse!

Mouse staggered to his feet
and ran all the way home.

"It's been a terrible day," he said to his mum
    as she bathed his cuts and bruises. "I fell into
        a hole, got wet in the river and—"
"Never mind, Son," said Mum . . .

"It could have been *much* worse!"